This Little Tiger book belongs to:

_____

_____

_____

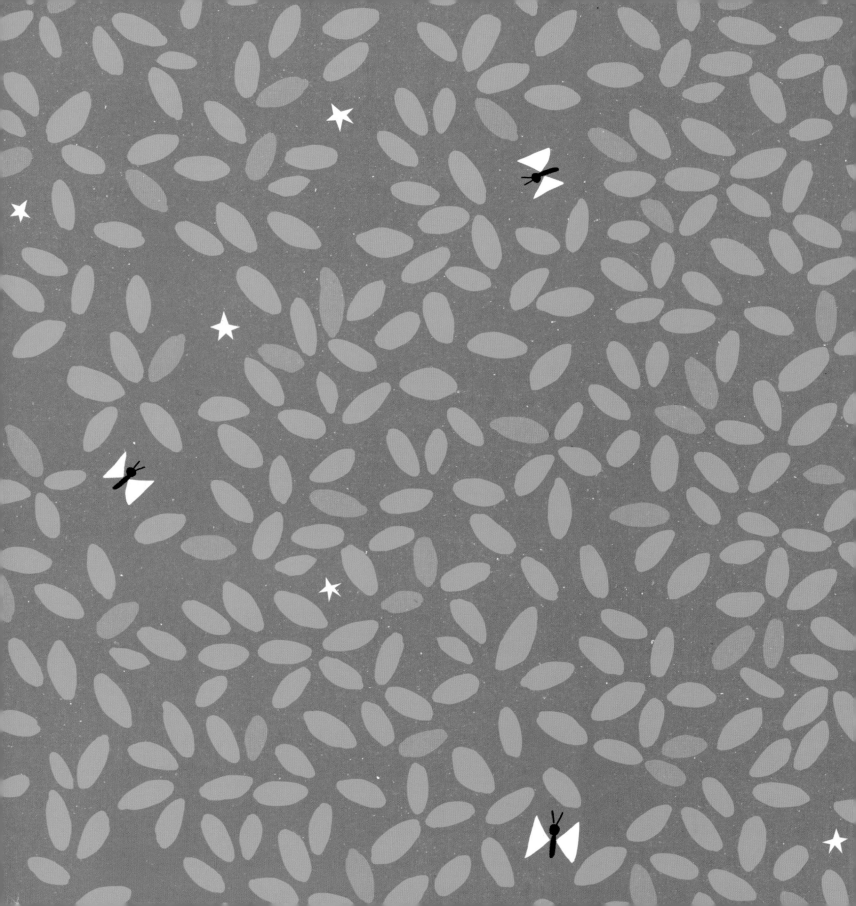

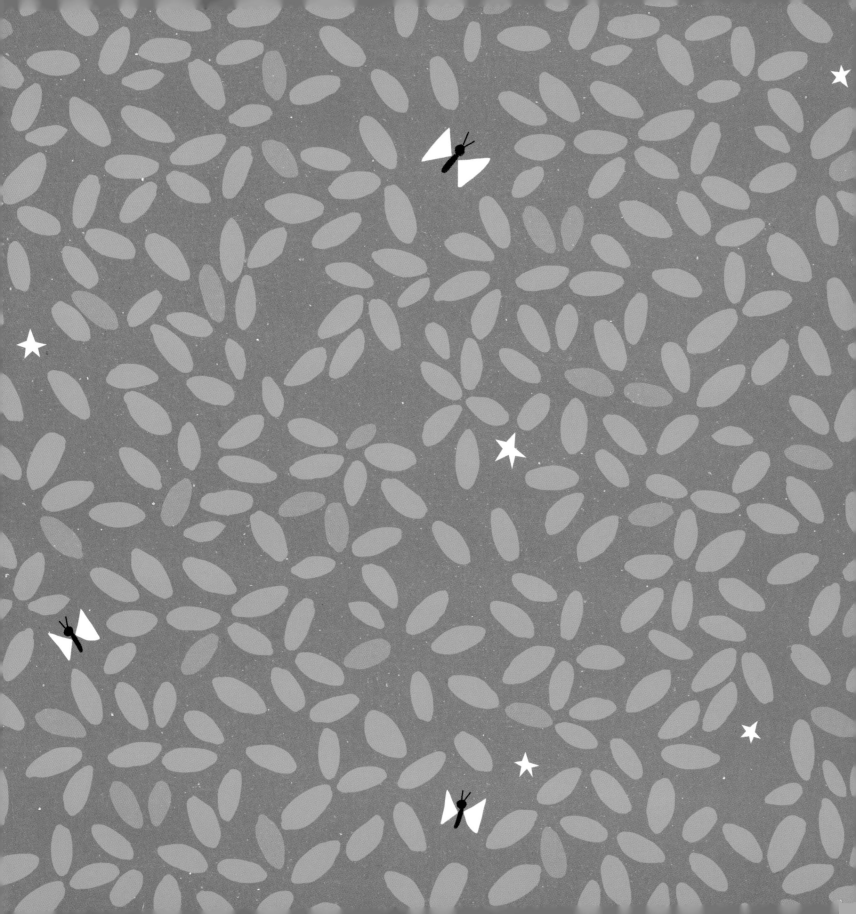

For Sasha
~ E. T.

For Etta, and her Mummy Owl x
~ G. D.

LITTLE TIGER PRESS LTD,
an imprint of the Little Tiger Group
1 Coda Studios, 189 Munster Road,
London SW6 6AW • Imported into the EEA by
Penguin Random House Ireland, Morrison Chambers,
32 Nassau Street, Dublin D02 YH68
www.littletiger.co.uk

First published in Great Britain 2017
This edition published 2020
Text by Georgiana Deutsch
Text copyright © Little Tiger Press Ltd 2017, 2020
Illustrations copyright © Ekaterina Trukhan 2017
Ekaterina Trukhan has asserted her right to be
identified as the illustrator of this work
under the Copyright, Designs and Patents Act, 1988
A CIP catalogue record for this book is available
from the British Library • All rights reserved

ISBN 978-1-78881-788-2 • LTP/2700/4000/0521
Manufactured, printed, and assembled in
Foshan, China. Fourth printing, May 2021
10 9 8 7 6 5 4

10, 9, 8...
OWLS UP LATE!

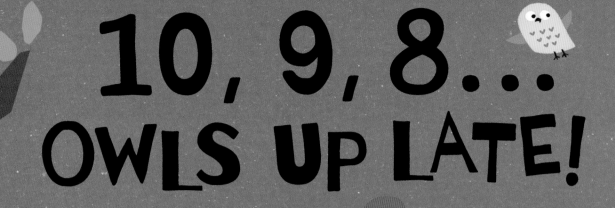

by GEORGIANA DEUTSCH

Illustrated by EKATERINA TRUKHAN

A COUNTDOWN TO BEDTIME

LITTLE TIGER

LONDON

10

TEN little owls were playing in a tree,
hopping and hooting happily.
From up in the branches
the silly owls said:
"We're having too much fun
and we won't go to bed!"

NINE little owls were singing in a tree,
twittering and tweeting tunefully.
From high in the branches
the noisy owls said:
"We're busy with our song
so we can't go to bed!"

EIGHT little owls were dancing in a tree,
wiggling and jiggling joyfully.
From up in the branches
the playful owls said:
"We're feeling much too bouncy
and we won't go to bed!"

SEVEN little owls were hooting in a tree,
chittering and chattering excitedly.
From high in the branches
the happy owls said:
"We're busy telling stories
so we can't go to bed!"

2 TWO little owls were jumping in a tree,
stamping and stomping stubbornly.
From high in their branches
the tired owls said:
"We want to stay up here
and we won't go to bed!"

ONE little owl was dozing in a tree,
snuffling and snoring sleepily.
He opened up one eye and
yawned as he said:
"I'm very sleepy, Mama,
and I think it's time for bed!"